D0476757

Note to parents, carers and teachers

Read it yourself is a series of modern stories, favourite characters and traditional tales written in a simple way for children who are learning to read. The books can be read independently or as part of a guided reading session.

Each book is carefully structured to include many high-frequency words vital for first reading. The sentences on each page are supported closely by pictures to help with understanding, and to offer lively details to talk about.

The books are graded into four levels that progressively introduce wider vocabulary and longer stories as a reader's ability and confidence grows.

Ideas for use

- Begin by looking through the book and talking about the pictures. Has your child heard this story before?

- Help your child with any words he does not know, either by helping him to sound them out or supplying them yourself.

- Developing readers can be concentrating so hard on the words that they sometimes don't fully grasp the meaning of what they're reading. Answering the puzzle questions at the end of the book will help with understanding.

For more information and advice on Read it yourself and book banding, visit **www.ladybird.com/readityourself**

Book Band

6

Level 2 is ideal for children who have received some reading instruction and can read short, simple sentences with help.

Special features:

Frequent repetition of main story words and phrases

Short, simple sentences

Peppa Pig and Suzy Sheep are playing tennis.
"To you, Peppa!" says Suzy.
"To you, Suzy," says Peppa.

6

7

Careful match between story and pictures

The girls cheer.
"Hooray! It is fair," says Peppa. "We win!"
Everyone loves football.

Large, clear type

28

29

Educational Consultant: Geraldine Taylor
Book Banding Consultant: Kate Ruttle

LADYBIRD BOOKS

UK | USA | Canada | Ireland | Australia
India | New Zealand | South Africa

Ladybird Books is part of the Penguin Random House group of companies
whose addresses can be found at global.penguinrandomhouse.com.

www.penguin.co.uk   www.puffin.co.uk   www.ladybird.co.uk

Text adapted from 'Peppa Plays Football', first published by Ladybird Books 2010
This Ladybird *Read It Yourself* edition published 2016
001

This book copyright © ABD Ltd/Ent. One UK Ltd 2016
Adapted by Ellen Philpott

This book is based on the
TV Series 'Peppa Pig'.
'Peppa Pig' is created by
Neville Astley and Mark Baker.
Peppa Pig © Astley Baker Davies Ltd/
Entertainment One UK Ltd 2003.
www.peppapig.com

Printed in China

A CIP catalogue record for this book is
available from the British Library

ISBN: 978-0-241-24438-8

All correspondence to
Ladybird Books
Penguin Random House Children's Books
80 Strand, London WC2R 0RL

Playing Football

Adaptation written by Ellen Philpott
Based on the TV series *Peppa Pig*. *Peppa Pig* is
created by Neville Astley and Mark Baker

Peppa Pig and Suzy Sheep
are playing tennis.

"To you, Peppa!" says Suzy.

"To you, Suzy," says Peppa.

George wants to
play tennis, too.

"You can't play tennis,
George," says Peppa, "but
you can be the ball boy!
You have to get the ball
for me and Suzy."

Peppa and Suzy love
playing tennis.

"Ball boy!" says Peppa.

George has to get the ball.
So he runs and runs.

George does not love tennis.

11

Peppa's friends are here.
They want to play, too.

"We can play football!"
says Danny Dog.

"Hooray!" everyone cheers.

Everyone loves football.

The friends get into teams.

They have a boys' team and a girls' team.

Pedro Pony is in goal for the boys and Rebecca Rabbit is in goal for the girls.

Richard Rabbit gets the ball. He runs and runs.

He kicks the ball past Peppa and Suzy Sheep.

Then Richard kicks the ball past Rebecca and into the net.

"Goal!" says Danny Dog.

"Hooray!" cheer the boys.

19

Rebecca Rabbit gets the ball.

She runs past Pedro Pony.
Next, she throws the ball
into the net.

"Goal to me!" says Rebecca.

"It's not fair," says Pedro.

"Rebecca does not get a goal," says Danny. "You can't throw the ball in."

Daddy Pig is here.

"I will help you," he says. "The next team to get a goal will be the winners."

Richard Rabbit has the ball! He runs and runs. Then he kicks it into Pedro's net.

"Goal! The boys win!" cheers Danny Dog.

"It's not fair," says Peppa.

"But the ball went into the boys' own net!" says Daddy. "So it's an own goal."

The girls cheer.

"Hooray! It is fair," says
Peppa. "We win!"

Everyone loves football.

How much do you remember about the story of Peppa Pig: Playing Football? Answer these questions and find out!

- Who is Peppa playing tennis with?

- Who is the girls' goalkeeper?

- Who scores the first goal?

- Who throws the ball into the net?

Look at the pictures and match them to the story words.

Peppa

Pedro Pony

Daddy Pig

Richard Rabbit

Danny Dog

Tick the books you've read!

Level 1

Level 2

Level 3

Level 4

Available on the App Store

ANDROID APP ON Google play

The Read it yourself with Ladybird app is now available